Oliver Moon's Fangtastic Sleepover

Sue Mongredien

Illustrated by
Jan McCafferty

USBORNE

For Joe Savage, with lots of love

First published in 2007 by Usborne Publishing Ltd., Usborne House,
83-85 Saffron Hill, London EC1N 8RT, England. www.usborne.com

Text copyright © Sue Mongredien Ltd., 2007

Illustrations copyright © Usborne Publishing Ltd., 2007

The right of Sue Mongredien to be identified as the author of this work has been
asserted by her in accordance with the Copyright, Designs and Patents Act, 1988.

The name Usborne and the devices ♀ ⊕ are Trade Marks of
Usborne Publishing Ltd.

A CIP catalogue record for this book is available from
the British Library.

UK ISBN 9780746084793 First published in America in 2011. AE.

American ISBN 9780794530945 JFM MJJASOND/11 01315/1

Printed in Dongguan, Guangdong, China.

Contents

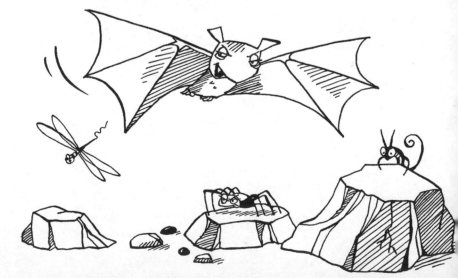

Chapter
One

"Come on, Mom, there's no need to *cry*,"
Oliver hissed. He gazed around the school
playing field, hoping that no one else
could see the way his mom's eyes were
glistening. "I'll be *fine!*"

Mrs. Moon sniffed and dabbed at her
eyes with a bright green handkerchief. "I
know," she said, pressing her lips together.

"But…" She shook her head. "I'm going to miss you, that's all."

"*Me* miss Ollie!" added the Witch Baby, Oliver's sister. She suddenly burst into noisy tears and threw her arms around Oliver's legs. "Come back, Ollie!"

"I haven't left yet!" Oliver said. He tried to step out of his sister's clutches, but she clung on even tighter. "And I'm only going for *one night*!" he reminded them.

Oliver sighed. He and his classmates were gathered on the field with their families, saying goodbye before setting off for the school trip. But nobody seemed to be making half as much fuss as his mom and sister!

Mrs. Moon blew her nose loudly. "Yes, yes, I know," she said. "I'm sure you'll have a great time. It's just that you've never stayed away from home before, so…" She took a deep breath, then put on a big fake smile. "Now – did you remember your toothbrush?"

"Yes, Mom," Oliver replied. "You asked me that five minutes ago, remember?"

"Come on, everyone," shouted Mr. Goosepimple, Oliver's teacher, just then. "It's time to fly!"

"I'd better go," Oliver said, prying his sister's sticky fingers off his legs. "I'll see you tomorrow, okay?"

"Do you have your lunch?" Mrs. Moon went on.

"Yes, Mom. Look, I've really got to go now, so—"

"And your pajamas?"

"Yes, Mom. So—"

"And clean underwear?"

Oliver gritted his teeth. He was starting to lose his patience. "Yes, I've got clean underwear!" he replied, rather louder than he meant to. Someone nearby snickered – Bully Bogeywort, it sounded like – and Oliver felt himself turn hot with embarrassment. Honestly!

"Oliver," Mr. Goosepimple called. "When you're ready...?"

Oliver looked around and saw that all his classmates were lined up in front of their teacher, astride their broomsticks. Everyone was waiting for him and, judging by their giggles and smirks, they'd all heard what he'd just said about his underwear. Typical! "Bye, Mom. Bye, Sis," he gabbled, kissing them both and then rushing to join his friends.

"Take care!" his mom called after him.

"Take CAKE!" his sister added in a bellow.

"And don't forget your clean underwear!" Bully Bogeywort said loudly, with a horrible grin. Oliver made a face at Bully, then kicked one leg over his broomstick, and lined up with the rest of his class.

"Everyone here? Excellent," Mr. Goosepimple said. "I'll just send all our bags on to the museum, and then we can be off. Leachville Haunted House Museum, here we come!"

Oliver felt a thrill of excitement as he and his classmates soared into the air and flew after their teacher. He'd never been on a school sleepover before! He'd been looking forward to it for ages, imagining telling spooky ghost stories with his friends, and having midnight feasts. "This is going to be so cool," he called across to his best friend, Jake Frogfreckle.

Jake grinned back. "It's going to be awesome!" he shouted. "I hope we see some spooks!"

Oliver nodded. "The spookier the better," he declared. Oh, he was so pleased that Mr. Goosepimple had chosen "Ghosts and Ghouls" as their class project this term at Magic School. He couldn't think of anything he'd rather be learning about!

Leachville wasn't very far from Cacklewick, Oliver's home town, and it only took the school group half an hour or so to fly there. After bumping down in the museum grounds, Oliver looked up at the towering stone building in front of him, feeling even more excited.

The Haunted House Museum was old and ramshackle, with ivy all over the front of it and big, dusty windows. Oliver knew it was really famous for all of the creepy creatures and spirits that lived there. Just gazing at it was enough to send a shiver down Oliver's spine. He could hardly believe they were going to be spending the night there!

"Here we are," Mr. Goosepimple said, patting his windswept hair back into place.

"Now, if you'd all like to leave your broomsticks over in the parking rack, we'll go inside."

Moments later, Oliver and Jake hurried up the stone steps at the front of the museum, with the rest of their class. There was a wide, stone porch area, big enough for them all to crowd onto. Mr. Goosepimple stepped forward to open the door, but as he reached out a hand to grasp the handle, the door slipped back with a loud creak, all by itself.

"Oooooh!" squealed Hattie Toadtrumper. "Did you see that, everyone?"

"Even the *door* is haunted!" breathed Colin Cockroach, openmouthed.

Mr. Goosepimple peered inside. "Anyone there?" he called. "Mr. Fungus?"

There was a deathly silence. Oliver
held his breath as he tried to see past his
teacher into the museum, but couldn't
make out anything in the darkness. Was
this definitely the right place? he
wondered. The building seemed deserted.

"Hello?" Mr. Goosepimple called again. He pulled out a flashlight from his cloak pocket and shone it around. Oliver could see thick cobwebs dangling from the ceiling, and a gleaming white skeleton in one corner. A couple of bats fluttered out of the door, making Pippi Prowlcat shriek as one swooped low over her head. Then…

"Boo!" came a loud shout.

Oliver almost jumped out of his skin, and both Pippi and Hattie screamed at the tops of their voices. "Aaaaarghh!"

Light blazed inside the museum suddenly, and Oliver could see a tall, bony-faced man in the doorway, cackling wheezily. "Oh, I got you there, didn't I?" he chuckled. "I got all of you, all right!"

Recovering himself, Mr. Goosepimple
switched off his flashlight. "M-Mr.
F-Fungus?" he asked uncertainly.

The man stopped cackling and grinned at them all. Oliver could see that most of his teeth were rotted away to nothing, and his cheeks seemed to have caved in. "Hello there. You must be the group from Cacklewick's Magic School, right?"

"Right," Mr. Goosepimple said weakly. He held out his hand. "Hamish Goosepimple, very pleased to meet you."

"Fergus Fungus, likewise," said Mr. Fungus, shaking hands. He narrowed his eyes as he looked around at the students, then stepped backward and held out his arm with a flourish. "Come in, come in... for the spookiest experience of your lives!"

Chapter
Two

His heart thumping, Oliver stepped into
the Haunted House Museum with his
friends. "Wow," he breathed to Jake,
staring around. Now that the lights were
on, he could see that the walls were
painted black, and hung with paintings
of ghosts and weird-looking creatures. A
couple of grinning skeletons dangled from

a hat stand, and a strange white shape kept whizzing around the ceiling, making an eerie, high-pitched, whistling noise.

"What's that, do you think?" Jake muttered, gazing up at it.

"Dunno," Oliver replied. "It's moving so fast I can't tell."

Mr. Fungus, overhearing them, beamed. "That's Archibald," he said. "He's our newest ghost. Gets a little excited when we have lots of visitors, that's why he's zooming around like that." He clapped his hands together with a loud crack, and the white shape stopped moving. "Archibald, calm down! Come and say hello!"

Oliver held his breath as the white shape swooped down toward Mr. Fungus and hovered just behind his right shoulder.

Archibald had a long, white, shimmering body and a mischievous glint in his eye. Before Mr. Fungus could say another word, Archibald zipped over to Mr. Goosepimple and was tugging at his beard.

"Hey, watch it!" Mr. Goosepimple yelled, trying to bat him away. Archibald dodged out of reach, and whizzed up to the ceiling again, cackling uproariously.

"Archibald, behave yourself," Mr. Fungus ordered the ghost. "Calm down!"

With a shrieking laugh, Archibald did a nosedive toward Mr. Fungus, whooshing straight through the middle of him, and out the other side! Oliver stared, fascinated. It was really weird the way the shimmering ghost could vanish into Mr. Fungus like that, and come out again.

"Stop that!" Mr. Fungus ordered, giving Archibald a swipe with his bony hand. Archibald made a rude face and went to rattle the skeletons. "I hate it when he passes through you like that," Mr. Fungus grumbled. "Nasty, 'orrible 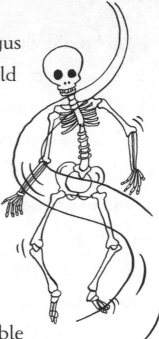 feeling, like someone's pouring cold water right through your belly." He wagged a finger at Archibald. "Naughty," he said. "Any more of that, and you'll be packed off to the dungeon, with Stink."

Mr. Goosepimple cleared his throat. "Shall we…start the tour?" he suggested, with a baleful glance at Archibald. "It sounds as if there's a lot to see in the rest of the museum."

"Of course," Mr. Fungus said. He gave one last look at Archibald. "Now, you be good. No throwing them bones around again, either," he added. He rolled his eyes at Oliver's class, and shook his head. "Took me ages to put them skeletons back together, last time he got in a huff."

Oliver was rather sorry to be leaving the mischievous Archibald behind – he was very entertaining! – but couldn't help feeling excited about what he'd see next. He and the rest of the class followed Mr. Fungus along a narrow, dark passageway. The floorboards creaked under their feet, and Oliver could hear a whirring noise.

Mr. Fungus led them into a large, hot room, and the whirring grew louder. Oliver blinked as he saw a swarm of strange purple and green creatures darting around above their heads. They were a cross between birds and bats, and zipped around so quickly, they seemed to blur into colorful streaks across the ceiling.

"Everyone in? Last person, shut the door behind you," Mr. Fungus ordered. "Quick! Before all of 'em escape!"

Lucy Lizardlegs slammed the door at once, looking nervous. "What *are* they?" she asked, staring up at the flying creatures.

"Jinxes," Mr. Fungus told her proudly. "Quite rare in this country, they are.

They're found in hot places, that's why we keep the radiator on all the time in here, so that they feel at home, like."

"Can I hold one, please?" Colin Cockroach asked.

Mr. Fungus shook his head. "Not likely!" he said. "You mustn't touch one, or you'll be jinxed with bad luck. Fearful bad luck, a Jinx can bring you!"

There was a nervous gasp from around the class, but Mr. Fungus only chuckled. "Oh, don't worry," he said. "They'll leave us alone. They don't like people. Now, these are your tropical Jinxes," he went on. "They eat glow-beetles and egg-worms. And if I need to handle 'em for any reason, say one of 'em's ill, I have to wear this special protective clothing" –

he gestured to a bright yellow boiler suit, helmet and gloves hanging up on the wall – "and use this Jinx net, to catch 'em." He pointed to what looked like a fishing net, propped up near the door. "So. Who's got a  question for me, about these Jinxes?"

Hattie Toadtrumper put her hand up, as did Carly Catstail. Oliver was just listening to Mr. Fungus explain how the Jinxes slept upside down like bats, when he felt a tug at the back of his cloak, and then something wiggly drop down his back.

Oliver let out a yell of surprise and spun around to see Bully Bogeywort guffawing, the Jinx net in his hand. "Unlucky for some, Oliver Moon!" he jeered.

"What?" Oliver cried, wrestling to get the wiggly thing out of his cloak. "Did you just drop a Jinx down my back?"

"Boy! Hey, you boy!" shouted Mr. Fungus, striding over to Bully. "What do

you think you're doing, young man?
Didn't you hear me say not to touch the
Jinxes?"

Bully was all wide-eyed innocence.
"Sorry, sir," he said. "I was just trying out
the net. I didn't mean to *catch* one. And I
didn't know it would fly down Oliver's
cloak like that!"

"It didn't fly down my cloak!" Oliver
said furiously. "*You* put it there!"

The Jinx shot out from under Oliver's
cloak just then, and silence fell as the
whole class watched it go. It was
dripping with a bright silver slime now,
and Mr. Fungus gave Oliver a
sympathetic look. "Oh dear," he said.
"Silver, eh? It got you, then, son. I'm
afraid you're in for some bad luck soon."

"Let's move on to another room," Mr. Goosepimple said nervously. "Bully – keep your hands to yourself from now on."

"Yes sir, sorry sir," Bully Bogeywort said. But when Mr. Goosepimple wasn't looking, he stuck out his big green tongue at Oliver.

Oliver scowled back at him, but inside he couldn't help feeling rattled. What was going to happen to him, now that he'd been touched by the bad-luck Jinx?

Chapter Three

"This way, this way," Mr. Fungus said, opening the door carefully and leading everyone out. Oliver followed, his mind in a whirl. Trust Bully Bogeywort to spoil the school trip for him when it had barely begun!

Jake elbowed him. "Cheer up," he said encouragingly. "We're going to the

Spook-Detecting room now. That's bound to be awesome!"

Oliver nodded, and tried to take his mind off the Jinx episode as Mr. Fungus went further along the dark corridor and opened a different door. This room had glass cases on the walls, showing all sorts of peculiar machines and pieces of equipment.

"This here is what we use for transporting the ghosts," Mr. Fungus said, pointing to a metal contraption with a long, rubber nozzle. "When it's switched on, this piece of equipment can suck up ten ghosts at a time, and keep them contained for up to a week." He patted one of the metal sides, with a faraway look in his eyes.

"We've had all sorts in here. The Headless Highwayman, we brought him down from Sludgely, when he was annoying the townsfolk. He loves it here in our museum, rides around outside in the garden most of the time. Who else? The Ghostly Giggler, the Cursed Cat…some real legends."

"What's this?" Lucy Lizardlegs asked, pointing at a large, black canister. It sort of looked like a fire extinguisher, Oliver thought, peering at it.

"Aha," Mr. Fungus said, rubbing his hands together. "That's our Draculator. Sucks up vampire bats, that does." He picked it up and showed them the "on" button. "Press that, and you can suck them right out of the sky. Got to catch

them before they transform, though.
Otherwise – forget it! They'll be after
your blood."

"Get many vampires in Leachville, do
you?" Mr. Goosepimple asked nervously.

Mr. Fungus looked solemn. "We used
to. Too many, if you ask me," he replied.
"Don't get me wrong, the bats are pretty

harmless. It's when they turn themselves into full-size vampires that the trouble starts. Nasty creatures!"

Oliver turned his gaze to a display unit showing both a vampire bat, with sharp fangs sticking out of its furry face, and a model of a full-sized vampire, too. He'd never actually seen a real vampire or vampire bat before, and he had no wish to meet either. Far too scary! The model vampire had a long black cape, slicked-back black hair and sharp white fangs, with blood dripping down from them. Oliver shuddered, and turned away at the sound of Mr. Fungus's voice again.

"Now it's time to move on to our Magical Collection room," he was saying. "This way!"

The Magical Collection room was a treasure trove of all sorts of interesting things. There were piles of books about ghosts, pictures of the museum from hundreds of years ago when it was just a haunted house, and lots of magical items connected with ghosts and spirits.

"Look! A mummy case!" Jake said in a hushed voice, nudging Oliver.

Oliver looked and saw a large, golden box standing on its end, with its door open. Inside was a model mummy, with bandages wrapped around its head and body.

"Wow," Oliver breathed, staring at it. Now that *was* spooky, he decided. He knew the mummy inside was just a model, but the thought of it striding around at night like a zombie…brrrr! It was definitely enough to give him the creeps!

"What's up? Missing *your* mummy?" came a sneering voice just then, and Oliver whipped his head around to see Bully Bogeywort's ugly mug behind him.

"Get lost," Oliver snapped. He still hadn't forgiven Bully for his trick with the Jinx. He really wasn't in the mood for any more teasing. In fact, he thought, as Bully strode away snickering, the only thing he *was* in the mood for was revenge. He had to get Bully back somehow!

Oliver watched thoughtfully, as Bully walked up to a stand holding a big spell book and leaned over it to read something. "Vampire-summoning spell," he said aloud. "Cool! I'm not scared of vampires – let's invite a few over!"

"No, don't!" Pippi Prowlcat squeaked. "There's no way I'm having a sleepover with a vampire!"

Bully chuckled. "You're a wuss," he said. "I could take on a vampire, no problem."

Meanwhile, Oliver's eye had been caught by an old-fashioned silver toasting fork, used for keeping werewolves at bay. He seized it impulsively. Right! Now to give his enemy a nasty shock!

Oliver marched straight over to Bully, intending to give him a good old prod with it.

Unfortunately, though, the bad-luck Jinx chose that moment to start working. Just before he reached Bully, Oliver

tripped on a rug and went crashing
straight into him, sending both of them,
and the spell book, flying to the floor.
Oliver's wand bounced out of his cloak
pocket and landed on the book, and the
toasting fork fell to the ground with
a clatter.

"Hey!" shouted Bully, getting up and
rubbing his big bottom. "Watch it!"

But Oliver wasn't listening. He'd just
noticed the way the page of the spell
book was glowing bright scarlet where
his wand had fallen on it. The words
Vampire-summoning spell had turned
thicker and blacker at the top of the
page, and a plume of horrible, smelly,
black smoke was spiraling up from
the paper and into the air...

"Whoa!" said Bully, staring. "What's happening?"

Jake ran over and slammed the book shut, ashen-faced. "Oliver," he said in a scared sort of a voice. "I think your wand might have just set off the Vampire-summoning spell!"

"What?" Bully yelped, not sounding quite so confident anymore. "Vampires? Do you mean…they're going to come here?"

Oliver edged away from the book uncertainly, as if a vampire might spring right out of its pages. He swallowed. "I don't know," he said, hoping he wasn't in for even more bad luck. "Surely you can't cast a spell just by dropping your wand on it, can you?" He hesitated. "Can you?"

Jake bit his lip nervously. "I'm not sure," he said. "I guess we'll have to wait and see."

Chapter Four

Oliver was glad to get away from the
Magical Collection room and have his
lunch, but he felt very edgy the whole
time, and couldn't help looking out for
vampires arriving at the museum. Oh,
how he wished he hadn't gone for Bully
Bogeywort with the toasting fork like
that! Why hadn't he been able to keep

his temper and ignore Bully's mean remark?

After lunch, Mr. Fungus had organized a ghost hunt around the museum for Oliver and his classmates, giving them all spotter sheets with pictures of the resident ghosts for them to mark off as they saw them. Normally, Oliver would have thoroughly enjoyed seeking out all the ghosts, but now he couldn't stop thinking about the vampire spell. The Jinx really would have brought him *terrible* luck, if it turned out to be true that he'd set off the spell by mistake.

Oliver teamed up with Jake for the ghost hunt and they set off around the museum. They soon spotted the huge

yellow Stink lurking in the dungeon,
Archibald (three times), the Headless
Highwayman
galloping wildly
around the back
garden, a Slurker
(a skinny, snake-like
ghost), and finally the
Ghostly Giggler, who
pointed at them both and
laughed. Every time they
saw a shadowy form in a
dark corner, Oliver's heart

jumped and he was braced for it to be a
vampire appearing…but to his great
relief, it was only ever more ghosts.

A great bell clanged throughout the
museum as Oliver and Jake were

finishing their drawings of the Ghostly
Giggler on their spotter report cards, then
they heard Mr. Goosepimple's faint shout.
"It's time for dinner now! Come down to
the entrance hall, we've ordered pizza!"

"Quick, let's get there before Bully
Bogeywort scarfs it all," Oliver said, as
he and Jake raced down the corridor
toward the hall.

A big, black tablecloth had been set out on the floor there, and some of the other students were already sitting cross-legged in a circle, munching pizza, as Oliver and Jake skidded in.

Oliver sat down, grabbed a slice of pus and pepper pizza and bit into it hungrily. Mmmm! Delicious!

"So, have you had a good time this afternoon?" Mr. Goosepimple asked, taking a sip of slug squash.

"Yeah!" the class replied as one.

"I think we should all give three cheers to Mr. Fungus for letting us come and see his ghosts, and explore the museum," Mr. Goosepimple said. "Hip hip…"

"HOORAY!" everyone yelled.

"Hip hip…"

"HOORAY!"

"Hip hip…"

"HOORAY!"

Mr. Fungus looked pleased. "I'm glad you've all had fun," he said. "And I'm sure you'll have a really exciting time tonight, sleeping down here. You can't beat it — waking up in the night to the sound of ghostly howls, or feeling the ghosts floating around you in the darkness, and—"

"Sounds…wonderful," Mr. Goosepimple said, passing a hand over his forehead. He'd turned a little pale and sweaty-looking, Oliver noticed, and kept glancing nervously around the room, as if he were expecting Archibald or another ghost to come whizzing in at any moment.

"Right!" said Mr. Fungus cheerfully. "Let's get these pizza boxes cleared away, and then we can get you all ready for your sleepover. You're going to love it!"

Oliver shivered. The sun was going down outside, and lamps flickered on around the hall as the museum started to get darker. He could hardly believe he was

going to be sleeping in here tonight –
with all the ghosts. He just hoped there
wouldn't be any *extra* visitors arriving...

Mr. Goosepimple waved his wand over
the pizza boxes. At once, the leftover
slices of pizza all flew into one box
and arranged themselves neatly.

The lid closed, and the box flew over to
a table at the side of the hall. Then he
waved his wand again, making the

empty boxes and the tablecloth vanish in a puff of black smoke.

"There," he said, and pulled out a jar of knitter-spiders. "Now, you all go and brush your teeth and put your pajamas on, while I get these spiders to whip up some hammocks for us all."

Oliver and Jake unpacked their overnight bags, and went off to the boys' bathroom. When they came back, the knitter-spiders had woven springy hammocks for everyone, around the hall.

"Goodnight, then," Mr. Fungus said. "My living quarters are upstairs. See you in the morning…and sweet dreams!"

A minute or so after Mr. Fungus had left the room the lamps went out without any warning, and the hall was plunged into darkness.

Pippi Prowlcat gave a scream. "Who turned them out?" she asked into the gloom. Her voice shook a little. "Was that supposed to happen?"

"Wooo-ooo-ooo!" someone called, in a ghostly voice.

"Who was that?" Pippi wailed. "Colin, was it you?"

"Woooo-oooo-oooo!" came the ghostly sound again, followed by giggles.

"Don't!" Pippi cried. "I don't like it!"

"It's only Bully messing around," came Hattie's voice.

"Nothing to do with me," Bully replied. "Must have been one of the ghosts!"

It wasn't long before there was a whole

chorus of ghostly wails and moans coming from the hall — and lots of nervous giggling! Oliver forgot the vampires in the fun and joined in, putting on his spookiest voice to try and scare his friends, and Jake told a great ghost story about a haunted castle, which had everyone squealing with fear.

"Come on, settle down," Mr. Goosepimple said after a while. He was in a hammock at the far end of the hall, away from the others. "Let's have some quiet, or we'll never get to sleep."

There was silence for a few moments. Then someone gave a tiny "Wooo-ooo!" and everyone cracked up laughing.

"Settle *down*!" Mr. Goosepimple snapped, sounding irritated. "It must be late, and I'm sure everyone's tired. It's time to go to sleep now. If there's any more messing around, I'll have to send people home with a Transporta spell."

There was silence after that. Nobody wanted to go home – they were having way too much fun!

Oliver lay awake for a while, tossing and turning in his hammock. One by one, his friends seemed to be falling asleep all around him, judging by the gentle snores and deep breathing he could hear. But Oliver didn't feel at all sleepy. Lying here in the inky darkness, he couldn't help thinking about the Vampire-summoning spell again. What was he going to do if vampires *did* arrive? And more to the point, what would *they* do to *him*?

Chapter
Five

Oliver was still awake when he heard
midnight chiming from somewhere in the
house. Archibald had whizzed in and out
a few times, shimmering in the dark, and
Oliver had seen the Slurker slither
through the hall, sniffing all the sleeping
students, but apart from that, the ghosts
had been quiet.

As he shifted around in his hammock for what felt like the hundredth time, Oliver saw the moon slide out from behind a cloud and a slice of silvery light fell through the open window. Then Oliver's eyes nearly fell out of his head in shock. For there, quite visible in the moonlight, was a whole swarm of bats flying toward the window – and flapping into the museum.

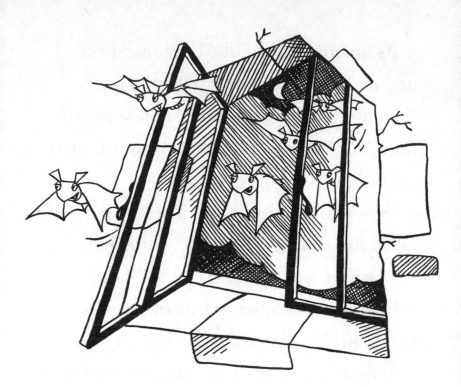

Oliver's eyes widened in horror as he
saw that the bats all had white fangs.
Vampire fangs! Oh, no. This was what
he'd been dreading. It seemed that the
Vampire-summoning spell really had
worked!

As quietly as possible, he leaned over and nudged Jake, who was in the next hammock along. Jake stirred and opened his eyes. "What's going on?" he murmured sleepily.

"Sssshhh!" Oliver hissed. Then he pointed up at the ceiling. "Look," he whispered.

The bats were circling the hall now, talking to each other in squeaky voices. Oliver held his breath while he listened.

"I'm starving, can't we start eating them now?" one twittered, its fangs gleaming in the moonlight.

"Mmmm, they smell so delicious," another replied.

The biggest bat spoke up next. "Let us transform before we dine," he suggested. "Follow me!"

The bats swooped after him, out of the hall and down a corridor. Oliver turned to Jake, his heart beating wildly. "Did you hear that?" he croaked.

Jake nodded, white-faced in the moonlight. "Vampires," he said. "And they want to eat us!"

Oliver groaned. "This is all my fault," he said. "I brought them here with the Summoning spell!" He could hardly believe this was happening. He sat up and wiggled out of his sleeping bag.

"I've got to stop them," he told Jake, "before they come back and start attacking everyone."

"But what are we going to do?" Jake whispered.

"I don't know," Oliver replied. Then something clicked in his mind. "Got it!" he hissed. "We'll suck them up with the Draculator! Remember Mr. Fungus showed us how to switch it on earlier?"

"Good idea," Jake said, sounding relieved. "Nice one, Ol. We'll have to be quick, though — we can only catch them while they're still bats, can't we? We've got to get to them before they transform. Come on!"

Oliver and Jake clambered out of their hammocks and tiptoed along the corridor that the vampire bats had just flown down. The stone floor was cold under their bare feet, and Oliver felt his arms and legs prickle with goosebumps.

The two boys ran silently down the corridor toward the Spook-Detecting room. They could hear the eerie whirring of the Jinxes as they passed their room, and mysterious creaks and rattling noises from elsewhere in the museum. "Here we are," Oliver panted as they got to the Spook-Detecting room. He pushed open the door and ran in, Jake close behind. There was the Draculator, all ready for action!

Oliver grabbed it thankfully, and then he and Jake raced out again. "Let's find those vampires!" he said, trying to sound brave.

He and Jake didn't have to search very far. As they left the Spook-Detecting room, they heard voices further along the corridor. The boys exchanged glances, and Oliver felt his insides lurch. He hoped they were in time to catch the bats. He really hoped they hadn't already transformed into full-sized vampires!

The door of the Magical Collection room was slightly ajar, and Oliver and Jake crept closer to listen.

"Now we shall dine," they heard a throaty voice declare. "Let's go and get them!"

Oliver took a deep breath, his knees knocking. *Here goes nothing*, he thought. Then he pushed his way into the room, brandishing the Draculator. "Not so fast!" he shouted.

Chapter Six

Oliver's skin prickled with fright as he saw what was inside the room. Not vampire bats anymore – but six full-sized vampires, with long, black capes and white faces. They were all staring straight at Oliver. He felt sick with nerves but continued to hold the Draculator up toward them, trying to look as threatening as possible. Maybe it could still do *something* to them, he thought hopefully. Maybe it would zap them or…

But an awful thing happened before he could even flick the machine on. The vampires all burst out laughing! Oliver's heart sank at the sound. The vampires didn't seem scared of the Draculator at all.

"That won't do anything," one of them scoffed. "It only sucks up vampire *bats*. You're not going to get all of us in there, not now we've transformed."

Oh, no! This was like a horrible nightmare! Oliver wanted to run, but his feet seemed to have frozen to the ground. He racked his brain frantically, but all he could think about was how big and sharp the vampires' fangs looked. Help!

"Now what?" Jake whispered from behind him.

Oliver dredged up every last drop of courage he could find inside himself, and took a deep breath. He was going to have to try to talk his way out of this now that the Draculator couldn't help. "Look, I'm really sorry I summoned you," he said to the vampires, his voice shaking on each word. "But it was an accident! I promise, I didn't mean to! So if you could all just go back to wherever it is you live…"

His voice trailed away as the tallest vampire folded his arms and glared at him. "*You*…summon *us?*" he scoffed. "You actually think that we vampires are controlled by mere…*boys?!*"

"Of all the nerve!" another one put in.
"We came of our own free will, pal!"

"Although we haven't had
a very nice welcome," the
tallest vampire said icily.
"First you think you
can summon us up for
fun, then you try to kill
us with that...thing!"
he went on, gesturing
to the Draculator
with a look of
disdain. "Well, that's just charming!"

"Like you weren't about to try and kill
us!" Jake burst out bravely. "We heard
you talking about how delicious we
smell!"

The vampire nearest them wrinkled

his nose. "How delicious *you* smell?" he repeated, looking appalled. "As if!"

"Don't flatter yourself!" another vampire said in disgust.

There was a pause while Oliver tried to make sense of this. "You mean…" He lowered the Draculator, feeling confused. "You mean you *don't* want to attack us? You're not going to…drink our blood, or anything?"

The vampires laughed and laughed. "No way!" one of them spluttered, still chortling. "That's so old-fashioned, you know."

"Totally unsophisticated, too," another sniffed. "We packed in the blood-drinking years ago. No, we came for the pizza. Didn't you know vampires love pizza?"

There was another pause. Jake stared. "*Pizza?*"

"Of course!" the smallest vampire said. He grinned. "As long as there's no garlic bread with it, of course. We're not so fond of that, funnily enough."

Oliver felt faint with relief. The vampires *weren't* on the attack. And this wasn't his fault. The vampires had come for the pizza, not because of any Summoning spell. "Well, if you're sure that's all you want..." he started.

"It is!" the vampires chorused.

"We want pizza," the youngest one said, his eyes imploring. "We're starving!"

"We might even forgive you for trying to Draculate us," the tallest vampire said, his lips twitching with amusement.

"I'm sorry," Oliver said, feeling hot with embarrassment. "I didn't know – I thought..."

The tallest vampire put a friendly hand on Oliver's shoulder. "Don't worry," he said. "No harm done."

"Th-thanks," Oliver stammered. "Um, the pizza is this way!"

Oliver and Jake led the vampires back down the corridor toward the main hall.

"So, what are you all doing at the museum anyway?" the lead vampire asked chattily. "We weren't expecting to see so many young wizards and witches in here."

Oliver explained about the sleepover. "Oh, and if our classmates look a little frightened of you, don't worry," he said quickly. "We'll tell them that you're friendly."

"They're all really nice," Jake said.

"Well, most of them," Oliver corrected, thinking of Bully. "There's one person who isn't very nice at all."

"Oh, really?" the lead vampire asked, with a sympathetic look.

"Yes," said Oliver, "but just ignore him if he starts being mean." Then a thought struck him. "Actually," he went on, "he was just saying earlier about how he wasn't scared of vampires, and how he could fight one any day."

"He said that, did he?" the vampire replied, raising his eyebrows. "Ahh. You'll have to point him out to me. I'll go and say hello."

They'd reached the main hall now, and Oliver and Jake led the vampires between the hammocks toward the pizza box of leftovers on the side. Oliver and Jake were tiptoeing, so as not to wake anybody up, but the vampires weren't being so quiet.

"Ooh, pus and pepper, my favorite!"
one of them cheered when Oliver opened
the box of leftover slices.

"Delish!" exclaimed another, sinking
his fangs into a piece.

"What's that? What's going on?" came
sleepy voices from the hammocks as
Oliver's classmates woke up. A couple of
people – Bully Bogeywort included – let
out screams as they saw the vampires
standing there in the moonlight with
tomato sauce dripping from their fangs.

Oliver hid a grin. "Oh, Bully, thank goodness you're awake!" he cried, pretending to be frightened too. "You have to save us! You said earlier you could take on a vampire, no problem, didn't you?"

Bully's mouth swung open. His eyes were full of fear, as the vampires all turned to stare at him.

"I…I…" he stammered – and then he pulled his sleeping bag over his head. "Mr. Goosepimple!" he shouted, sounding terrified. "Save me!"

Mr. Goosepimple shifted in his hammock and sat up, rubbing his eyes. "Everything all right?" he murmured groggily. Then he saw the vampires.

"Help!" he screeched, leaping out of his hammock in fright.

Oliver tried not to laugh. "Don't worry, sir," he said. "They just wanted a midnight feast with our leftovers."

"They're really friendly," added Jake.

The lead vampire winked at Oliver. "Any friend of Oliver and Jake is a friend of ours," he said with a meaningful glance at Bully's sleeping bag. "Sorry for disturbing you all, anyway. We can't resist pizza, you see!"

"Oh," said Mr. Goosepimple, recovering himself. "Well…in that case, help yourselves!"

Oliver grinned, as the vampires started chatting with his friends, between mouthfuls of pizza. What an amazing school trip he was having! He'd spotted all sorts of ghosts, he'd made friends with some vampires – and best of all, Bully Bogeywort had made a complete fool of himself in front of everyone. All in all, this was turning out to be one *fangtastic* sleepover!

The End

Join Oliver and his friends
for more magical mayhem at

www.olivermoon.com

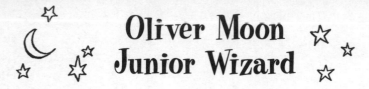

Oliver Moon Junior Wizard

Collect all of Oliver Moon's magical adventures!

Oliver Moon and the Potion Commotion
Can Oliver create a potion to win the Young Wizard of the Year award?

Oliver Moon and the Dragon Disaster
Oliver's sure his new pet dragon will liven up the Festival of Magic...

Oliver Moon and the Nipperbat Nightmare
Things go horribly wrong when Oliver gets to look after the school pet.

Oliver Moon's Summer Howliday
Oliver suspects there is something odd about his hairy new friend, Wilf.

Oliver Moon's Christmas Cracker
Can a special present save Oliver's Christmas at horrible Aunt Wart's?

Oliver Moon and the Spell-off
Oliver must win a spell-off against clever Casper to avoid a scary forfeit.

Oliver Moon's Fangtastic Sleepover
Will Oliver survive a school sleepover in the haunted house museum?

Oliver Moon and the Broomstick Battle
Can Oliver beat Bully to win the Junior Wizards' Obstacle Race?

Happy Birthday, Oliver Moon
Will Oliver's birthday party be ruined when his invitations go astray?

Oliver Moon and the Spider Spell
Oliver's Grow-bigger spell lands the Witch Baby's pet in huge trouble.

Oliver Moon and the Troll Trouble
Can Oliver save the show as the scary, stinky troll in the school play?

Oliver Moon and the Monster Mystery
Strange things start to happen when Oliver wins a monster raffle prize...